The Elephant in the Spring

celebrating similarities – for interfaith families

Suzan Loeb with **Lucy Ravich**

Archway Publishing books may be ordered through booksellers or by contacting:

Archway Publishing
1663 Liberty Drive
Bloomington, IN 47403
www.archwaypublishing.com
1 (888) 242-5904

Because of the dynamic nature of the Internet, any web addresses or links contained in this book may have changed since publication and may no longer be valid. The views expressed in this work are solely those of the author and do not necessarily reflect the views of the publisher, and the publisher hereby disclaims any responsibility for them.

Any people depicted in stock imagery provided by Thinkstock are models, and such images are being used for illustrative purposes only.
Certain stock imagery © Thinkstock.

ISBN: 978-1-4808-4894-8 (sc)
ISBN: 978-1-4808-4895-5 (hc)
ISBN: 978-1-4808-4896-2 (e)

Print information available on the last page.

Archway Publishing rev. date: 8/4/2017

"We believe teaching the religious aspects of holidays is the responsibility of parents and their clergy. The intent of this book is to recognize the similarities of some traditions that are observed and honored during Easter and Passover; to make children of interfaith households feel more included and special; and to help raise awareness and understanding in all children. By promoting sensitivity and concentrating on similarities the goal is to unite – and dispel differences that divide."

Suzan and Lucy

Dedicated *(again)* to
Jared, Emma, Alexandra, and Eloise
Jenn & David, Greg, Alyson & Tyler
– and those two treasured friends
who continue to Believe...

and to
adults who grew up in interfaith households
(who wish they had a book like this
when they were growing up...)
and today's children of interfaith families
(who do!!)

These two holidays take place each year, some time during the Spring

Let's look at them and discover the fun and good times they bring

Both celebrate Nature –
each has a long
and rich history

Can you name which
they are and help solve
this great mystery?

You know them –
remember – think hard
now – use all of your might

Did you say, "Easter and
Passover"? Good job –
Yes... You Are Right!

Both of these holidays,
    filled with yummy things
    to eat and drink

Share several similarities –
    probably more than
    you think

Some years they happen
in early Spring, some
years they happen late

On our American Calendar
neither has a specific date

The Sunday after
    March 21st and the
    very next full moon

But no later than April 25th
    is when Easter
    sings its tune

Passover is the 15th to the 22nd in the Hebrew month of Nisan

But *our* Calendar shows us the dates so this holiday we won't be missin'

In other languages these holidays are known by very similar names

Hebrew's Passover is "Pesach", Latin's Easter is "Pascha" – almost the same

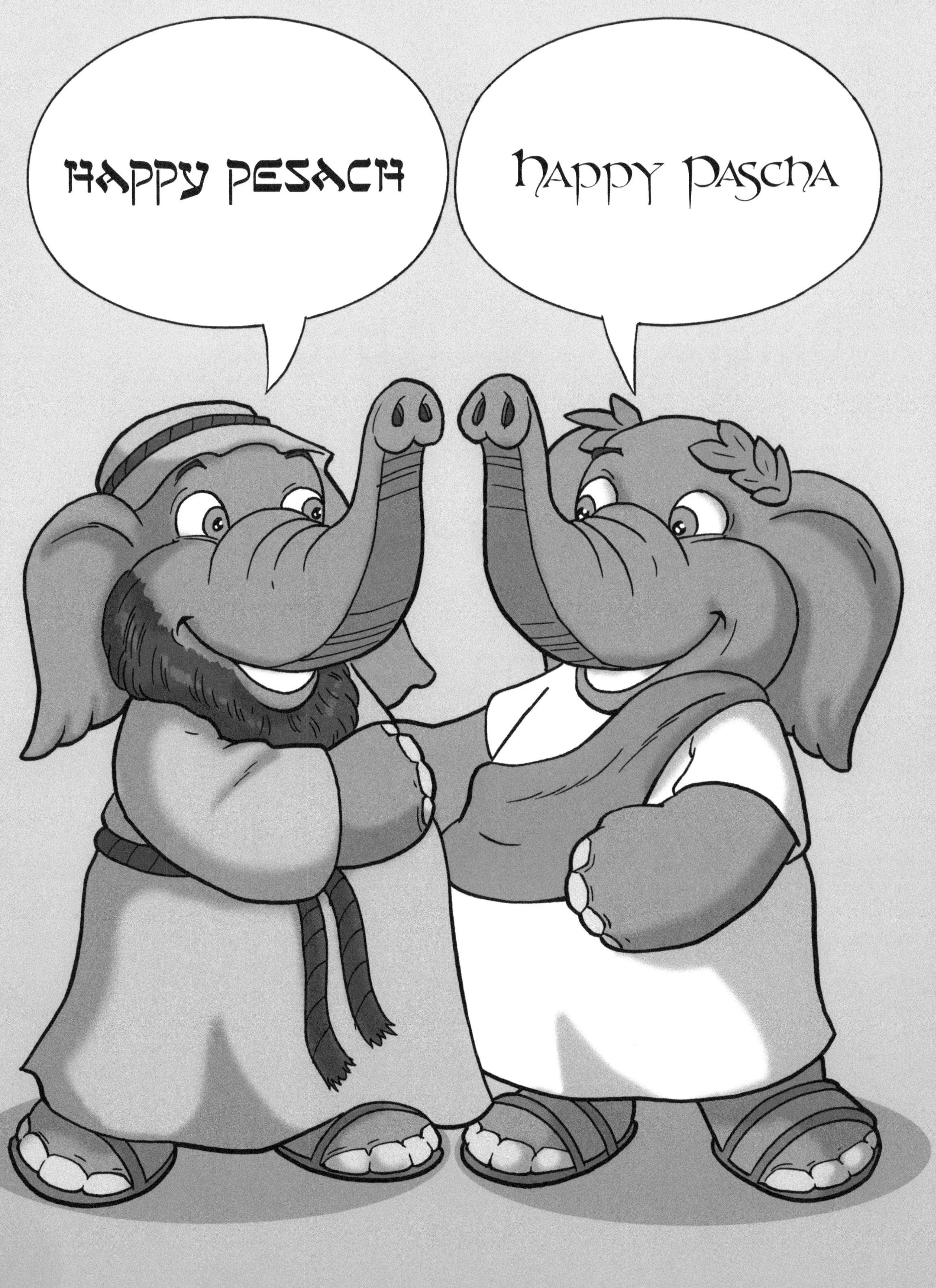
HAPPY PESACH
HAPPY PASCHA

Before Easter begins
you might give up
something you really like

And when the 40 days
of Lent are over
enjoy it again with delight

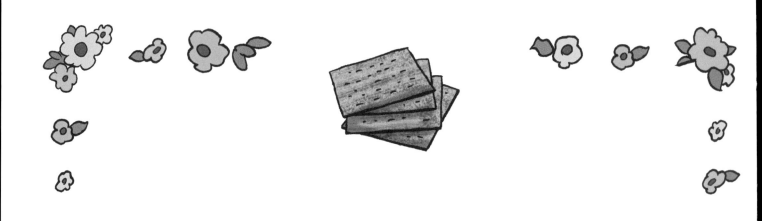

You also give up certain
foods during Passover's
8 nights and 8 days

Eating only things that are
produced and prepared
in very special ways

Family and friends gather
on Easter Sunday
to enjoy a festive meal

Everyone feasts together
sharing love and the
special bond they all feel

Family and friends gather
for Passover "Seder"
to enjoy a festive meal

Everyone feasts together
sharing love and the
special bond they all feel

At Easter children search
for hidden eggs that are
dyed and decorated

And are given Easter
Basket Gifts when all the
eggs have been located

During Seder children search
for a piece of matzoh
that's been hidden

And to the lucky one who
finds the "Afikomen",
a gift is given

Chocolate bunnies,
marshmallow chicks,
jelly beans, Deviled Eggs
and ham

Can all be found at Easter -
along with Hot Cross Buns,
yams and lamb

Chocolate covered matzoh
and macaroons, honey
cake and sponge cake too

Matzoh kugel and matzoh
brei are Passover
goodies, to name a few

These holidays send messages of Hope as we watch Nature revive

With new beginnings, buds, trees and flowers – the Earth again comes alive

If you are fortunate enough
to celebrate both of
these great holidays

Enjoy!

And remember Easter
and Passover are alike
in many, many ways

Two Recipes to Make, Share and Enjoy

(supervision of a responsible adult as needed)

Easy Deviled Eggs

6 eggs
¼ cup mayonnaise
1 teaspoon yellow mustard

2 pinches of salt
1 pinch of ground pepper
paprika to decorate the eggs

Remove the shells from 6 hard-boiled eggs
Cut each egg in half lengthwise
Remove the yolks from each egg and mash
Add mayonnaise, yellow mustard, salt and pepper
Fill each egg white with the mashed yolks
Sprinkle with paprika and place them on a serving tray

Easy Matzoh Brei

4 full pieces of matzoh
½ cup of warm water
4 eggs

2 pinches of salt
2 tablespoons of butter and oil
some sugar to sprinkle

Break the matzoh into small pieces in place in a large bowl
Pour the warm water over the matzoh to soften
When softened, drain off the water
Add the eggs and the salt and mix together
Heat the butter and oil in a frying pan
Pour the mixture into the pan
Fry each side until golden
Place on a platter and sprinkle with sugar

Howdy!

We first met in "The Elephant in the Room"

I'm so happy to see you again this soon

I'm here to help you prepare to celebrate

Two Spring holidays I think are just great

Passover and Easter...and I'm glad to say

You're so lucky to celebrate both - HOORAY!

Special times with family - pleasant traditions

Friends and festive feasts are bonus additions

We have so much in common, so much to share

Let's spread love and hope to everyone everywhere

Enjoy both holidays and the joy they both bring

With hugs and kisses from me -

The Elephant in the Spring

The Elephant in the Room
a holiday tradition for interfaith families
Suzan Loeb with Lucy Ravich

The Elephant in the Spring
celebrating similarities - for interfaith families
Suzan Loeb with Lucy Ravich

Color Me

Color Me

Color Me

CPSIA information can be obtained
at www.ICGtesting.com
Printed in the USA
LVHW07s1424030418
572131LV00022B/279/P

9 781480 848948